is to be returned on or before
mped below.

MAX'S DREAM

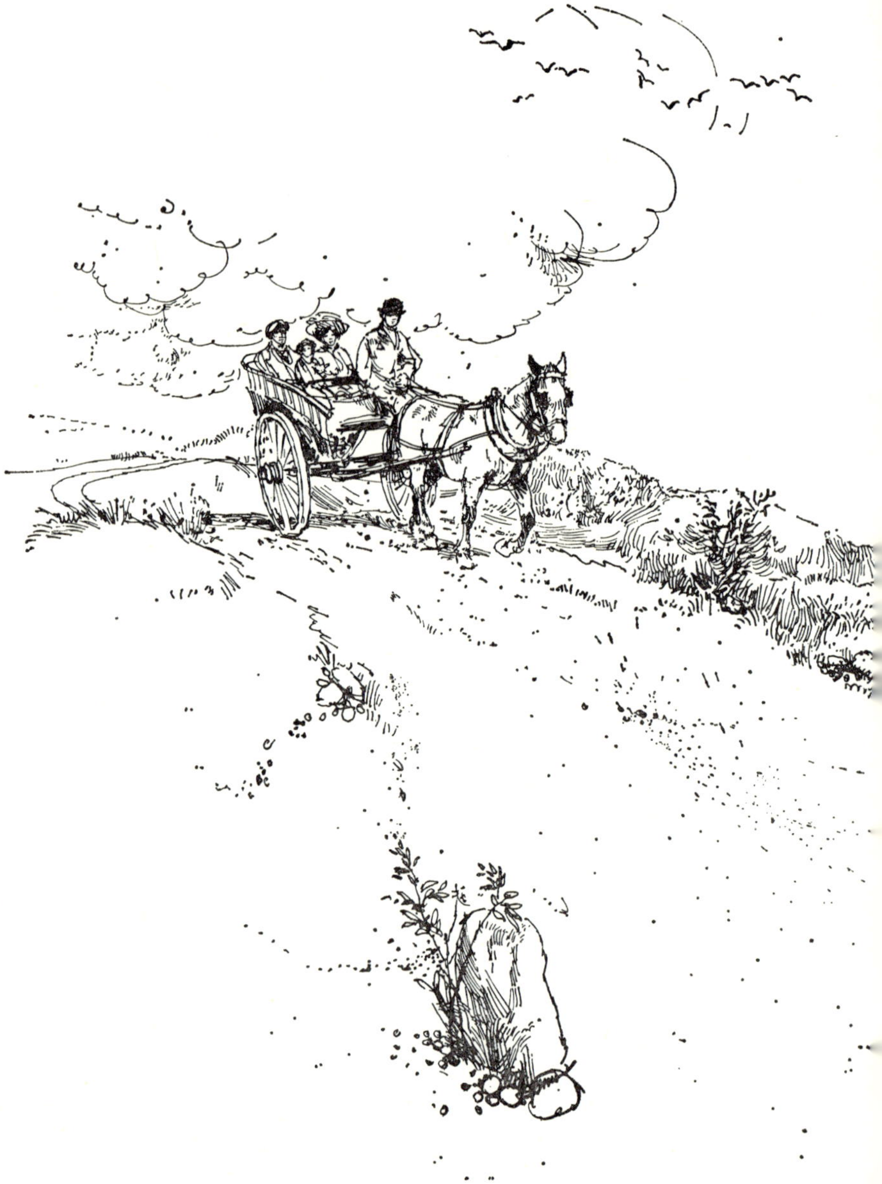

MAX'S DREAM

WILLIAM MAYNE

Illustrated by Laszlo Acs

HAMISH HAMILTON
LONDON

Text © 1977 William Mayne
Illustrations © 1977 Laszlo Acs
All rights reserved. No part of this
publication may be reproduced, stored
in a retrieval system, or transmitted,
in any form or by any means, electronic,
mechanical, photocopying, recording, or
otherwise, without prior permission in
writing from the Copyright holder.
First published in Great Britain 1977 by
Hamish Hamilton Children's Books Ltd
90 Great Russell Street, London WC1B 3PT
ISBN 0 241 89546 4
Printed in Great Britain by
Ebenezer Baylis & Son Ltd
The Trinity Press, Worcester, and London

To
Robin
Lindy
Janet
Penny
and Kristina Cockbill

ONE

I be an old woman now: but I was a young girl then, and my heart was full of love. I don't recall whether I was twelve or thirteen, or whether it was 1898 or 99.

The year don't matter. It was an April afternoon, springtime, and a warm day. The smell of the bread-and-butter flowers, the hawthorn, come into the room so strong it give Max a headache, and he put down his book, where he was lying, and put up a thin hand to his eyes and ask me to close up the window.

"I think I'll take some water and a little of the white powder," he said. "Just a little dusting on top of the water, Katie," he went on, when I was at the window and putting it to.

From the window I could see down to the school, and the children were coming out. Most of them run off in every way there was, and the master close the door to behind them just as I latch up the window. He done it to get the noise out the place, and I done it and got the noise out too. So it was quiet inside. I think it come quiet outside too.

There was three boys that might be scamps mostly, Trombo and David, and my brother Warren, that wasn't running, but walking along calm, and there was a funny touch to what they done, like setting their collars straight and dabbing at their boots with their elbows, setting up smart. Now there was three girls too following of them, and then they all come up together and talked a bit.

Oh, I say to myself, a bit of courting going on, and I think they might be lucky to be free for it, because me, I just had to love silent, and I couldn't get courted. So I see all this, and then come away from the window and get Max his cup of water, and sprinkle the bit of powder on it and stir up with the spoon, and he take it and doesn't say thank you or smile or nod, but drink it down and put the cup back in my hand and I put it on the table and the spoon in it.

"You're a kind girl, Katie," he said, but he doesn't say more to it that he might, such as he might like me or care a little, because I be just a serving maid in the house.

So he lies there and close his eyes, but it wasn't sleep yet. That comes in a bit after the white powder, and before that his pain goes.

I come to the window again, because I heard boots setting their way across the garden path, and I like to see what goes on. I thought it was more than boots of one person, and perhaps the donkey got in the garden again, and I would have to catch it and put it out on the heath which is what the house stands in.

I saw the donkey out among the furze bushes, so it wasn't him. Down below, outside the front door, I saw those three girls from school, Susan, Hannah, and little Ruth, and there was someone knocking at that door, but not them, they were standing too far out, and I see the tops of their heads.

I might go to the door when 'tis knocked at, but knocking means it's a ghost, or something important, or a stranger, because what we do out in these country places is open the door and call inside for folk.

Mrs Veary went to the door herself, and there she was talking to them out there but I can't hear what. It's the boys, I think, and those little maids coming with them. Then they all step in the house and I don't know why and I wished I'd got to the door first to learn about it.

Mrs Veary come up the stairs, and in at the door quietly.

"My," she said, "'tis warm here, and the window shut too."

"I closed it, Mrs Veary," said Max, but he meant more like that I closed it for him, because he couldn't raise from his bed.

"If you're awake, m'dear," she said, "there's a little deputation down below would like to see you."

"Who deputed them?" said Max, which was his way of talking.

"I don't know for that," said Mrs Veary. "'Tis just a word that fits from my side, and I know my words don't always fit from your side. But I think they brought themselves, and they would like to see you."

"I will receive them," said Max. "I'll sit up more, and open the window again, Katie."

So Mrs Veary sits him up and I open the window. But I like to help him, and she could have opened the window instead.

Mrs Veary went away down the stairs again, and I hear them all come up after her, like it might be the donkey trespassing proper, and then they all troop in the room.

"You'll have to stand," said Max. "The chair is Katie's." So I think, he cares for me before them at least.

So they stood, and it was who I thought, the boys Trombo and David and Warren, and the three girls. They hadn't a word among them at first, and then they push Trombo forward a bit, and he looks at the floor and he looks at the window and he looks at the cup on the table. Then he comes out with it.

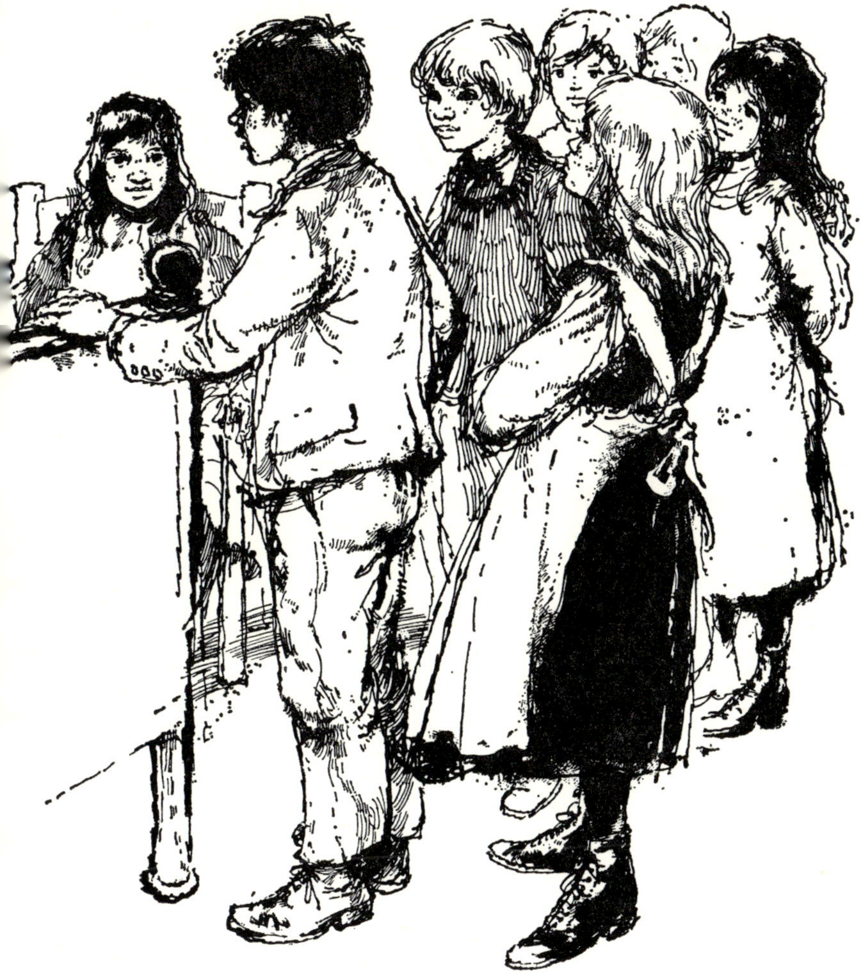

"We want you to be king," he said.

The others all looked excited at that, and pleased, and they need him to say yes at once, because we all knew what Trombo mean, but Max don't.

"I don't understand you," he said. "Has something happened to Queen Victoria?" I think that was a joke, because I know he wouldn't think he was to be king of the country, but of something else.

"'Tis our village game time coming up," said Trombo. "Out on the heath we have this game marked out."

"It was always there," said David. "We dance there at midsummer."

"I cannot dance, you know," said Max. Indeed, it pained him to sit up as he was now, but today he had taken the white powder and felt nothing.

"Well, 'tis made for you," said Trombo. "The king don't dance; he goes in the middle, and we all dance to him and put the crown on him and on the queen, and so 'tis."

"The place is called Troy Town," said David. "'Tis all marked out in ditches and walls, and 'tis a rare time and a feast after that you would be king of."

"Troy Town," said Max. "I have heard of that."

"Aye, 'tis famous in these parts," said Trombo. "They come from all the villages to see the king and queen and the dancers."

"There is a queen too?" said Max.

"We choose the king," said Trombo, "and we thought to choose you; and the king choose the queen, and that is any girl you like."

"Then I will choose a queen and be king for you," said Max. I hope then, and I think then, that his eye might come across to that chair he said was Katie's chair, and I thought he might say now it was Katie's throne. But maybe he don't see it, for his eyes close and that's sleep come to him after the white powder.

"I will," he said, and the eyes open a moment more, "choose," and then sleep is on him.

So there was no more to be said. The three little maids bring forward little posies of flowers and set them in the cup on the table that he drinks from, and it was disappointment to them he hadn't picked them same as they picked the flowers, but he is asleep.

"Tell him," said Hannah, "those are mine, and these are Ruth's, and these one's under are Susan's," and I say I will say, but there's no telling with them all in one bunch now.

They went downstairs again with Mrs Veary, and she told them that when he wakes he will choose a queen, and off they go, and I go to the gate after them to put the bolt on to keep that donkey out.

The children went off. They don't know all they want to know, but Max can't help that.

Then I was in the kitchen with Mrs Veary.

"Will he be able to go to Troy Town?" I asked her.

"The boys have a plan for that," said Mrs Veary. "They will take him along gently in the donkey cart."

"That might take them the whole day," I said. I was peeling potatoes at the time.

"That donkey is all nuisance and no pull," said Mrs Veary. "No, they will haul the cart themselves, and that will be less trouble than the donkey. They know work jades it. And which of you will be the queen to him?"

I feel foolish then, and I blushed over my potatoes, and of course she see that and laugh at me, but I don't mind Mrs Veary. She's one of us, after all, and don't harm, I think. But what I think don't cease my blushing for me.

"He has a choosing," I say, "and 'twas those three little maids brought flowers, and I've to tell him which is which when they're all mixed up."

"But he doesn't know them very well," said Mrs Veary. She was rubbing fat into flour for the pastry as she spoke, looking up and smiling friendly to me, and her fingers going rub, rub, rub, just the tips of them, and there I was clumsying about with the great old potatoes in the dirty water.

"'Tis most likely to be you," she said, finishing her mixing and rattling her fingers together over the bowl.

"It might," I say.

"But he might feel obliged to them," she said. "He was shown them to choose from, I'd say."

So I cut a potato in two to show what I thought of that, and she says not to take it to heart too much, because being queen isn't all, even being queen to him, and then we both thought about him. I think she wondered how he came to be in her house so long and what she should do about it because there wasn't anything; and I wondered if he would ever notice me, and how he had got to the house at all. Until then I had never properly thought about it.

We had pie to our tea, and she took his up, and brought it down again later and nothing of it did he touch, it was all cold on the dish as we had laid it hot.

"'Tis one of those bad nights coming," she said. "I'll sit by him until early morning, and then you come in, and when you go home tomorrow you can rest there," and that is the best we can make of it.

We knew his bad nights, when he could have no ease and his stomach would be ailing him and he would weep and hate his body for paining him and being of no other use.

By the time I come to sit with him with just a candle at dawn he was sleeping easier, just waking once and having to be attended to before the sun come in the room and I puffed the candle out and saw the shadow of the smoke on the wall. Then he takes a little milk through the morning, and rests and looks at the ceiling, and the smell of the bread-and-butter bush come through the window again, and the sound of bumble bees flying in and tasting it.

Mrs Veary gets up late, and I takes my dinner with her

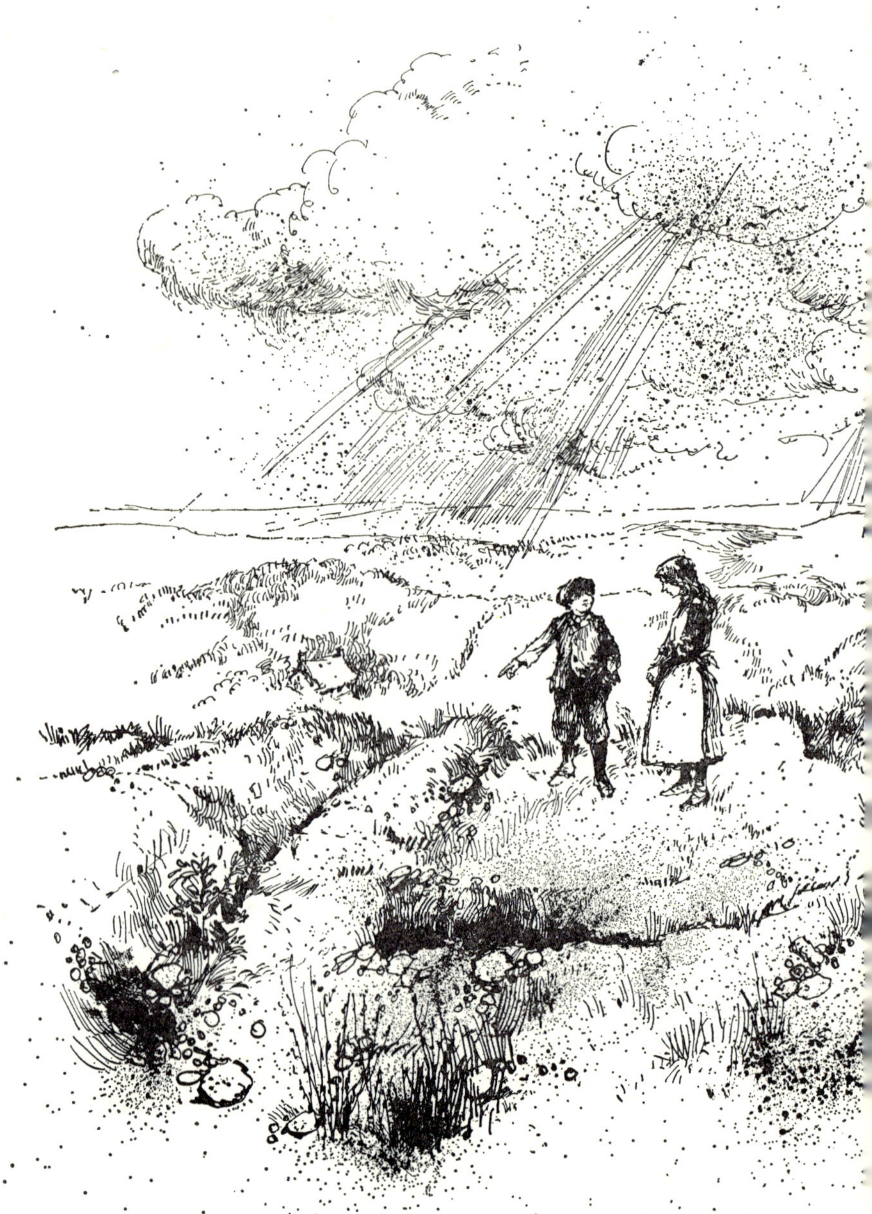

and then go home, and it's as she says, I falls asleep by the fire there until Warren skirmishes in and wakes me from my nap.

"Which of them is it?" he asks.

"He's been poorly since," I said. "He took one of his bad turns all night, and done nothing this morning before I left, just sit with his eyes open."

Then I was all hampered with being sat so long, and went out on the heath with Warren, not meaning to go anywhere but walk around and perhaps see if there was any lizards come out of the ground in the day. Then perhaps Troy Town was in our minds, and we got across that way and looked at it, a big old tangle of ditches dug out of the ground.

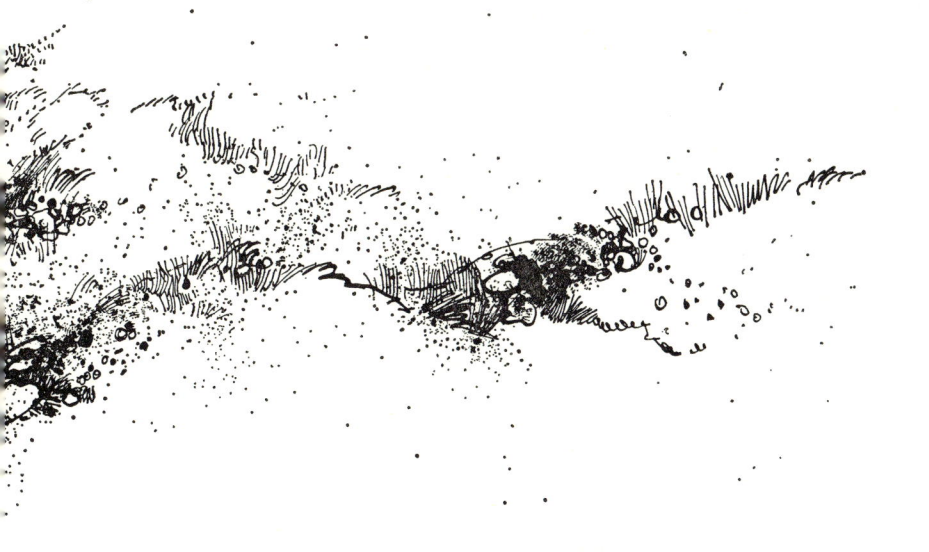

"How did they think of it?" said Warren. But of course we don't know that. For us it was just there, and you don't go in it except to dance at midsummer, unless maybe a ditch has to be digged out a little or one of the banks mended. We went all round outside it, and the sun come round at the back of us and send our shadows near across it, because the shadows were as long as a garden.

Then it was all shadow and no sun, and we come home and to our tea.

"Trombo been in," said our mother. "I told him he hadn't been fit to make a choice yet, and he say it doesn't matter just yet."

"Those three little maids be out of sorts with worry," said Warren. But I thought four maids were out of sorts with worry. For what I looked at most at Troy Town was the place at the middle where king and queen would sit, and I only want one way of filling it, not any choice of three others.

Warren come along with me when I went back to Mrs Veary's. "Just to hear he might have chosen," Warren said.

We went in the back door, and Mrs Veary was by the fireside with her mending.

"Asleep then," I said, seeing she was not up with Max.

"Both awake," said Mrs Veary, "If he wants he'll call or drop a book on the floor."

"He never said, then?" said Warren.

"About the queen?" said Mrs Veary. "Well, 'tisn't to me he has to say it but to some other lady," and I hoped the fire blushed my face enough for nothing to show on it. "You could go up and ask him, but go soft in case he's asleep."

We come up the stairs quiet and into the room. Max was reading by the candle. "You've been home," he said. "I smell your fireside on you. Good evening, Warren."

Then he come to the end of a word and closes the book.

"We just been up Troy Town," said Warren.

"I fell asleep yesterday," said Max. "I could not help it. Tell me what it is like. Does it have houses, and towers, and gates; ramparts, walls and battlements?"

"'Tis marks on the ground," said Warren.

"Look under the hearthstones," said Max. "I have read that treasure is often hidden under hearthstones."

"No sir, no hearthstones or anything of that," said Warren. "'Tis a turny trick of ditches all round one place and that be where the king and queen sit, and we wondered if you'd choosed yet which of they for queen."

"I did not know they had brought me flowers," said Max.

"I was to tell you which was which," I said. "But Mrs Veary took them from the cup and upset the order when she put them in the glass."

"They thought you might choose by them," said Warren.

Max looked down at the foot of his bed. "I have not chosen one of those," he said. "Not Hannah, not Susan, not Ruth."

"If that's what you say," said Warren. But I leap up inside myself, and what's left but me? So I wait for him to say, and what he said is that he has chosen some other girl, not any he knows here, and he will tell me or Warren when she has agreed. Then he says Warren had better go now, and when I had seen him to the door I was to come back.

Warren and I come down again, and I put him out the door at the back and bolt up the gate after him.

"He knows best," said Warren. "He's bound to know best, being like he is and such a gentleman person over us heath folk." But Warren didn't think it was right to have all three girls scorned. And I, I could bear to have them scorned, or I could bear not to be chosen myself, but I did not like it to be that no one of us was chosen.

So I came in and did not go upstairs again at once, but sat with Mrs Veary for a while by the fire.

" 'Twas not you he picked," said Mrs Veary. She could tell.

"I do not mind that," I said, and there was no blush in me about it.

"Hannah is a blithe little maid," she said. "Was it she?"

"No," I said. " 'Twas not she."

"Pretty Susan, then," said Mrs Veary.

" 'Twas not by looks," I said.

"Little Ruth would suit a crown on that dark hair," said she.

The tears come from my eyes and I telled her.

TWO

I don't tell her all I felt. She sit there criss-crossing her threads on the mending, slow and slow when the needle come through the strands and then quick and quick when she turn her wrist and pull the thread through and then slow and slow again when she hook the needle about and come in the other way and then jump on its neck again and pull back the other way, like she was following it not moving it. I don't darn like that ever in my life, just cobbling up for me.

"None of you," she said. "I made sure it was bound to be one of the three because they were brought to show, and if he wasn't having them it must be you." And she lays the needle under her other thumb and drops the scissors flat on the darn and trims off the thread, perks a look at the darn and puts all away.

I hanged the kettle over the fire and we had a cup of tea and then it's time for bed.

"I should have gone up again," I said. "He told me to."

"Morning will do," said Mrs Veary. "And maybe 'twill be a different thing by then. Warren will tell them what Max has decided, and they could decide something different in turn, like not having him in the affair at all."

"Or they might come and ask him to think on it again," I said.

"He's no great changer of his mind," said Mrs Veary. "And maybe they aren't either; so we'll see what come of it all."

So I say goodnight, and she's a kind person and she give me a hug and say it's not my worry, but of course she doesn't know, I think, or does she, because next she says, "Now don't have foolish fancies, Katie Katharine," which is what she calls me in friendly way.

So, well, I go to bed, foolish fancy and all.

Morning time come along, and it's so pretty in the time of year that I forgot what's in my mind about me and the others until I have the grate cleaned and the fire lit and the oven on drawing for making bread. I was just going out for some firing, and Mrs Veary is up with Max, when little Hannah comes up to the back door. She got her nanny goat with her taking home to milk, tight by the collar to stop her taking off the tops of the roses, bad as the donkey.

Warren must have gone home last night and never sent no news round, because she was asking "Has Max choosed yet? Which one is it to be?"

So my heart goes lump down again. "'Tis none of us," I said.

"It can't be Mrs Veary," said Hannah, "for she's a grown woman, and there isn't no one else."

"There must be," I said sharpish, "because 'tis another he have choosed, whether we like or no."

"Who can it be?" she said, she shook her head, and the goat shook her head and made for the honeysuckle and they drag each other off down the path, and I get the firing I come out for.

I come up to Max later for his tray. Up to the minute I open his door I was angered with him, and then I see him reading and I can't anger any more. I wish I know how it came I should love him, because first along he was Max that was lying there crippled in his bed day and night and it was pity-caring until it changed to love-caring, like Mrs Veary said, a foolish fancy because, like Warren said, he wasn't village folk.

He finished his words and looked up. He'd slept out well and looked fair, so I say, "You've slept well."

"Too well," he said.

I tell him there can't be too well in sleep, for if you're in it you can't tell.

"But I can tell, Katie," he said. "There was no dream."

There's dreams, I say, and there's fancies, I think, and one is the waking side of the other, so I am not happy with what I think. But I take up his tray.

"It was a very important dream," he said. "Put the tray down and sit in the chair, Katie. I want to tell you about it."

I do as he says. I can wash his dishes later, and I suppose the oven will go on heating.

"I had a dream," he said. "Not last night, because I

had no dreams last night, but the night before. I dreamed I was going over a moor, like the heath, and the road went on winding up and up until I got to the top, and then I went down the other side, and it was a very steep road down, and then I came to a river and there was no way across, so I had to go on further and further, and it wasn't moorland any more but green fields and I could see over the hedges and banks, until I came to the end of the river, and there still wasn't a way across, so I had to go in a boat."

I thought then it was like the ferry to Burmouth, which I went over when I was a little girl, but there stands a

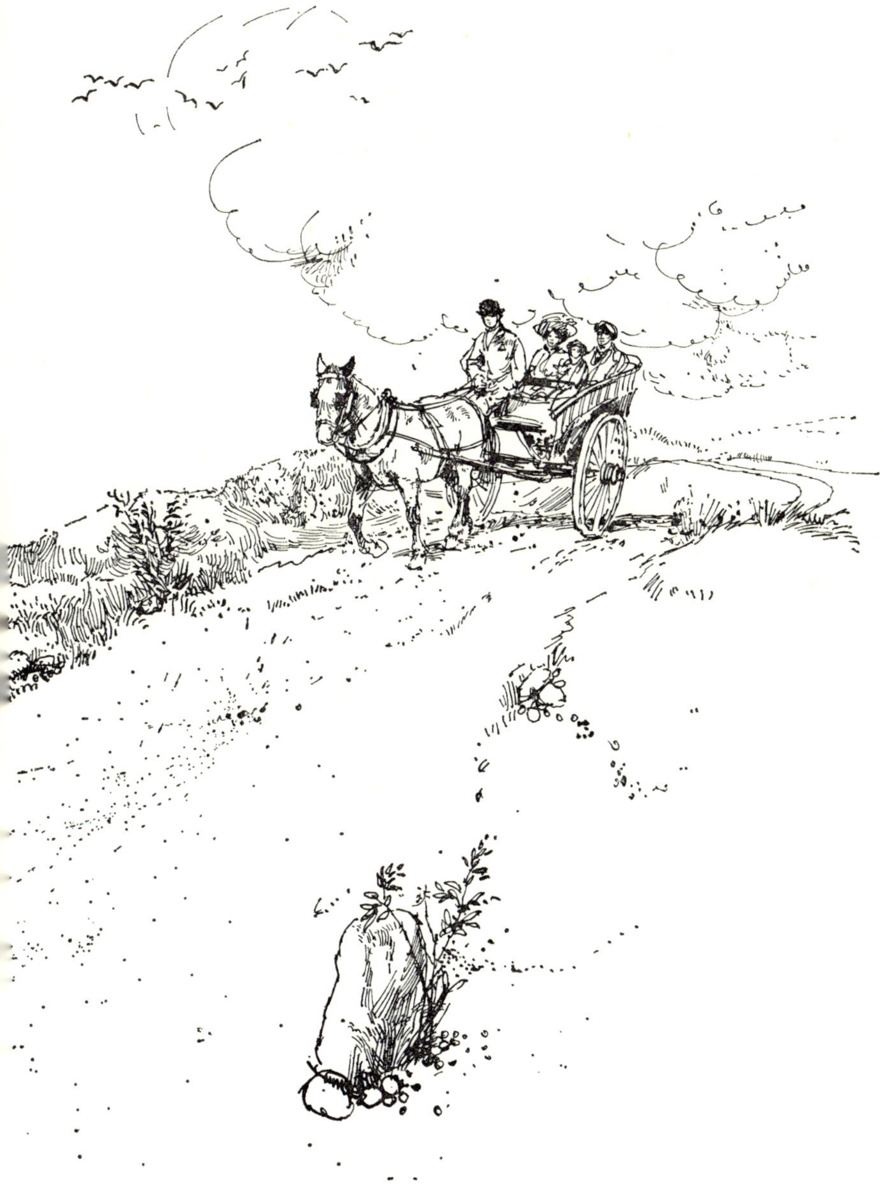

bridge over the place now, and a penny to pay for the cart as you go, which is cheaper than the ferry and you can take the cart with you for the market. But I didn't break his dream then with that.

"Then there was a town," he said. "All with painted houses."

Well, that was Burmouth, surely, and I told him so.

"We make dreams of what we see," he said. "But I was never in Burmouth. I was always here."

Now, that wasn't a fact, but perhaps he hadn't thought of that at all. But more of that comes later in this tale, so I'll leave it now.

"It wasn't Burmouth," he said. "It was a dream place that I haven't been to either."

"Was there sea?" I said.

"There were ships on it," he said. "Not like the ferry."

Burmouth, I said to myself, and then Sandmouth, and then the sea. If he never come there then Mrs Veary spoke of it sometime and that's what dreamed out.

"There were ships," he said. "But I didn't come near most of them, just to one. I don't know about ships, but this one was very clean and I could smell the paint."

Then I thought he was remembering the bread-and-butter flowers scenting through the window that had given him the ache in the head.

"I sailed in the ship," he said. "It wasn't like the ferry. It went into waves on the water and moved about."

That was the paddle-steamer to Swanston, I think, but I let him tell on, because this was no journey he made since he come here to Mrs Veary's. Because he wasn't always there, not right from the beginning.

"I came to an island," he said. "There was a house on it, a big one, with a great garden."

And there I don't know where he is, because Swanston was never like that, so it must be some other place or this was purely dream.

"I can't tell all the feelings in a dream," he said. "It was full of feelings, not like being alive but bigger. What you see in a dream is like part of you, all the trees are like your own hands and all the ground is like your own feet and the sun is part of your own eyes. There were trees in the garden, but their shadows were just as important; there were birds flying in the air, but the air was just as important. I can't tell you how it was all perfect and couldn't be different. Inside the house there was gold and silver in the hall and not any dust, and chairs that never got sat in and tables that never did anything, and a fire in the hearth, like a fire that was alive on its own and never had to be tended."

I thought of my fire down by the oven, and I hoped Mrs Veary was tending that, or the bread would be slow. But I couldn't make to leave Max then in the middle of the dream. He lie there and think about it for a bit, and I wait.

"There was another room," he said. "It was good and bad. There were two big boys sitting in it. They were doing something like playing a game, but it wasn't that. Maybe they were putting something together, but I couldn't understand it. It was more like a game. Then there was an old man in the middle of the room and he was making things with tools, and when he had made them he gave them to the boys and they played with them. He had white hair, and I think he was making things out of the gold like the gold in the hall. But that was all somehow bad, and I was frightened by it, because I understood it and I didn't understand it, and I didn't want to see so many people and I was afraid they would all talk to me and make me play the game and I didn't know how. But there was a good thing, and that was a girl sitting on a couch, and she leaned forward and I went to sit beside her because I wasn't frightened by her. Somebody said she would give me a kiss, and she was doing that when a lot of other noises came in as well as the voice saying she would kiss me, and the noises grew louder and were things like the garden gate and the school bell and the door closing and the fire being shaken downstairs and then I was awake and dreaming at the same time, and then I was just awake."

"That would be when I popped down to the fire that morning," I said. "When I come back you'd woke and I popped down again for some milk."

Then downstairs Mrs Veary call up for me to look at the oven again, and I say I have to go, if that finish the dream for now.

"That was the dream," said Max. "But Katie, that's the girl I want to be queen to my king for Troy Town. So I want to dream again and find her out."

I go down then, Mrs Veary calling louder, and I take the tray with me, and what with getting more firing and drawing up the oven again I get all hot and bothered with work and don't have time to think of the dream until dinner. And then, well, I can make nothing out of it, but I can't blame him for a fancy for it won't be any wilder than my own ones. But how he come to choose a girl in a dream I don't know then.

Trombo come up the house when he get out of school.

" 'Tis turmoil down there," he said. "Those little maids set sobbing all three most the day and wouldn't tend their lessons, and they gone home with stingers on their hands from the master's rule, and, well, it seems we done the wrong thing fixing on him up there for king, and 'tis only causing offence."

"So what do you come up for," I ask him. "I didn't get choosed neither, so your long face be no good to me."

"Maybe we ought to back out of choosing him and take another," said Trombo. "That would put us out of our calamity."

"You can't do that," I said. "You've to abide with what you said, and you know that."

"But if he won't choose," said Trombo, "then he isn't taking up his side of the bargain, and he has to do that."

"For that," I said, "he has chosen, and what's more he telled me of his choice, so he has took up his side of the bargain, so you must stay by yours." And then I close the door against his face and go back in the kitchen.

Then I felt real foolish, and the right opposite and contrary of a dream for nothing I could see about me belonged any more; I see my own things I had done, like the bread cooling on the shelf on its edge, and it don't have any part of me in it, and that isn't true; and I see the fire and that sat there neither part of me nor yet its own self, and that was never fire; and I think the air don't touch me no more, like I've come outside everything, and I go out of the kitchen and out of the door and catch up to Trombo at the gate.

"I be going," he said. "But what be I to say to my men?" For in this romp at Troy Town boys become men and little maids are women, to get them nearer the next up, the king and queen.

There stood his men, Warren and David, and apart stood the three girls, waiting for him.

"Now then, wait," I said, and I run back in to Mrs Veary in the parlour where she's doing nothing for a bit.

"What is it, girl?" she said. "You look so agitated."

"Just to go out for a bit, Mrs Veary," I said, "to talk to Trombo and them, because you don't know what Max did, he upset them once and then he had a dream and upset them twice."

"But he's been asleep all afternoon," said Mrs Veary.

"Yes, dreaming," I said. "And 'tis all to put right."

"Then go off for an hour, Katie," she said. Then she tell me to come back calmer, and off I go. I hanged my apron on the gate as I went.

It was two camps waiting out on the heath, the camp of girls blaming the boys for forcing them to have Max as the king, and the camp of boys looking at the girls and wondering why they were none of them fit to be chosen as queen. I was between them, and my pride was worst treated of all.

"Did he say any more?" said Trombo.

"He's asleep," I said. "Dreaming, most like; and that's what I come out to you for."

When I come out I was set to mock the dream rather, but then that seemed difficult and the same as hating, and that wasn't where I would be at all if I could help it. I knew Max must be right, and I knew Trombo and Warren and David thought when they come up to his room that he would be right, so right he was to be. We went a bit away from the house and sat down among the furze bushes.

"What's dreaming to do with it?" said David. "We can all dream."

So I tell them the dream, and it sounds bare, a little list of words and there won't come a meaning from it. But it has the girl in it, and that's what they want to hear, but they can make little out of it.

"Dreams are dreams," said Hannah. "I dream of dogs." So then we have a clatter about dreams that come to us, and then we get back to Max's dream.

"All these rivers and that," said Trombo.

"The ferry," I said, "where the bridge is by Burmouth. I thought I could begin to break his dream there, and then all the painted houses in Burmouth, and the ships at Sandmouth, and then I couldn't break it because the next ship, well, I thought 'twas the Swanston paddle-steamer, but it got to another place."

"'Tis Burmouth," said Trombo. "'Tis broken so far for sure."

"And what then?" said David. "Can we break the rest?"

So it went steady and easy, and I don't know all the time where I be walking, but it come to them if they break the dream then they find the girl for him, and no trouble. And those little maids as happy about it as Trombo and his men; and as for me, I'll do all for Max, whatever it wants to be.

Then Ruth thinks we should see her mother, and we just wait a while for Hannah to unpeg the goat and lead that along too, and we go to Ruth's place.

The dream come on by itself, I don't know we had to ask, she just told us, what wasn't nothing much but we never had it to consider before, and when she tell us I think, well stupid, you know all this without being telled of it.

"Little Max," she said, "he come here with his Mam and Da about eight years since and all lodge to Mrs Veary's, and he was lame then as he be lame now, no more, no less, for 'tis no worsening thing but fixed as long as he lives. Of course he went to Burmouth, for he be bound to have come that way at least to get here. 'Tis said, but of course I be no party to the deeds of such high folk, that he was come here to see some physician in the town to get a cure. But nothing came of that. The Mam and Da went down to take up a lodging in Fore Street, but they hadn't taken the boy down for 'twas the summer of the fever, and they were to come back for him. But they never come back, no, nor sent word, and there's the boy with Mrs Veary to this day, neither kith nor kin to him and no reward for that attention. We heard no more of them, and that be all I know. But that Mrs Veary is a very well-disposed person, and I do hear if she hadn't the boy burdened on her she might have had an offer made to make her happy since her own man died. But as it is she can't listen or hope."

Then I run back to the well-disposed person, who was sharp with me for overstaying a full extra hour I hadn't noticed.

THREE

And there was my apron still on the gate next morning, soft with dew, and the goat or that donkey patched a corner off and a black shell-slug riding up the back of one of the strings that was trailed on the ground, and I was in some slight trouble with that.

Mrs Veary drop in a black mood with me, and I drop in another, and she won't let me up to Max just as I am, like a thunder, she said, for that would upset him. I'm that black I don't love no one, and that was a weary day. Then I get the apron washed next morning and the slug-trail off it, and the black unpicks from my back, and I don't notice but I begin to sing again and Mrs Veary smile at me when she hears. So I get to see Max again, and I think what a foolish maid I be to dump down in such a state and not care even for him.

Warren and Trombo come up one night and Mrs Veary let us be in the kitchen.

"There's nothing done," said Trombo. "All very well to talk and listen, like to Mrs Cantle" (who be Ruth's mother), "but that don't bring us no nearer our queen."

"His queen," said Warren.

I wonder who wants his queen, except Max; and then I know I've to do everything for him, what puts him in my way and what puts him out of it, for all I have is fancy to live on, and over-plenty of that, eating all one dish day after day.

"We've broke his dream," I said. "So far."

"Did you know a dream come true?" said Trombo.

"Did you know a true come dream?" said Warren. A fun boy is Warren, and 'tisn't all who could follow him, like the time in school he come on this times table thing, right down in that simple one, two times two is four, and, well, he can't get over that nohow, it took hold of him right there in school and he won't say nothing else all day, and he won't stop shouting of it out in the class and laughing it was the humourist thing out, and I don't know what he thought, for it wasn't the proper arithmetic of it. For him it was no two and two the same, but different twos and twos each time he said it, or the same ones different ways round, and it come to blows with the master at last.

So he put the two matters about now, and there was sense, for the dream wasn't to be before the thing, but the thing must have come before the dream. Max had dreamed true, and we knew it all along or we couldn't have begun breaking the dream.

Trombo thumped Warren a bit for saying it so clear, because that be easier for Trombo to do than think out and speak. But after that, when I had them quiet again or Mrs Veary would put them out, we settled to think what to do next.

The next was to go down to Burmouth and Sandmouth and see what the next part of the dream was, for it was no dream but remembering. Only dreams don't every time speak the truth quite, because the night I left the apron on the gate I never dream of it, only a bunch of white flowers, but in the end the same thing.

Here we are, stuck on the heath, and there Burmouth do lie, ever so far apart. And then no way to know what to do if we come to Burmouth, just the three of us.

We come a bit more forward in the kitchen, and it grew dark and Mrs Veary sent them away, and coming forward a bit we still got nowhere.

"What's his name?" I said to Mrs Veary, when we had our cup of tea last thing.

"Spencer," she said. "Don't you know?"

"'Twas out of my mind," I said. She might have told us all we wanted to know, if we'd thought to ask, but it never come to our minds to question face to face up there on the heath, for we wasn't trained in the proceeds of gossip yet.

We did it our own way. The next bit drop in our hands easy again, just sat about and listening as we were. Next day was Sunday, and I go off home in the morning and get to church with Mam and Dad and Warren, and Warren run off round the church to get in the choir and my Dad go off up in the galley with his fiddle and my

Mam and I stay down below and there's the service, and it seems I don't listen.

Then my Dad goes off, and my Mam, and all of them and it come the time for Sunday School, and I have the little ones, and they're good today, 'tisn't often so. Parson get up at the end and said the trip come next Saturday, and we all be pleased at that and troop out before the blessing, so we never get it.

I have to hurry back, the dinner's to help with. But Trombo and Warren catch up to me at the gate.

"No time to play now," I said. "'Tis a foolish time to think of it, Trombo."

"No playing," said Trombo. "'Tis the trip, Katie."

"So," I said. "I don't aim to sit with you, Trombo, for you'll be up to tricks all day long. I be going to sit with my little ones, for their tricks don't shame folk."

"'Tisn't that neither, Katie," said Trombo.

"'Tis a marvellous thought," said Warren.

"'Tis the same trip each year," I said; but it seem then we might be talking of different things, so I let Mrs Veary cook on a bit alone and listen to them.

The thought come to Ruth first, and she tell Susan but it take a bit of time to sink in Susan's noddle, so Ruth tell Hannah while Hannah was wondering if to take her goat to the seaside, but I don't criticize stupid nor foolish. So they tell Trombo, who won't take sense or nonsense from a girl, but he take this, and tell me.

Naturally, we get a day in Burmouth next Saturday, and a ride each way in the charrybang, and what else do we want, why nothing, just made for us it is.

So I come to Mrs Veary too cheerful by a long shot, and she says I never was so up about the trip before, and why so now? And I wonder why, for the other girl is to be found at the end of it, just next Saturday, and that thought I dread and don't like to let it come at the end of doing everything for Max. But I've to know, I've to find out, and come Saturday I'm to break the dream whether or no I like it.

Only it turn the other way in a minute or two, when I get the baking dish from the oven, and my thoughts about this way and that I tips it over and teem out gravy on my foot, and the leg of lamb walks across the floor and I sit down and the dish goes to glory down among the ashes.

There come a bad place on my foot from that, and terrible pain. I got scolded, but I eat a little bit of dinner sat with my foot in a pail of water, and a blister rise up like a Yorkshire pudding and red all round.

"Two's no more trouble than one," said Mrs Veary. "You take to your bed the rest of the day." She think maybe I'll go home, but I think maybe I won't, I seen my Mam once or twice this week and that'll do.

I don't walk far for a few days, my ankle being up so in size. There come a bad night, and Mrs Veary sit up with me some of it, and then there come a worse one and

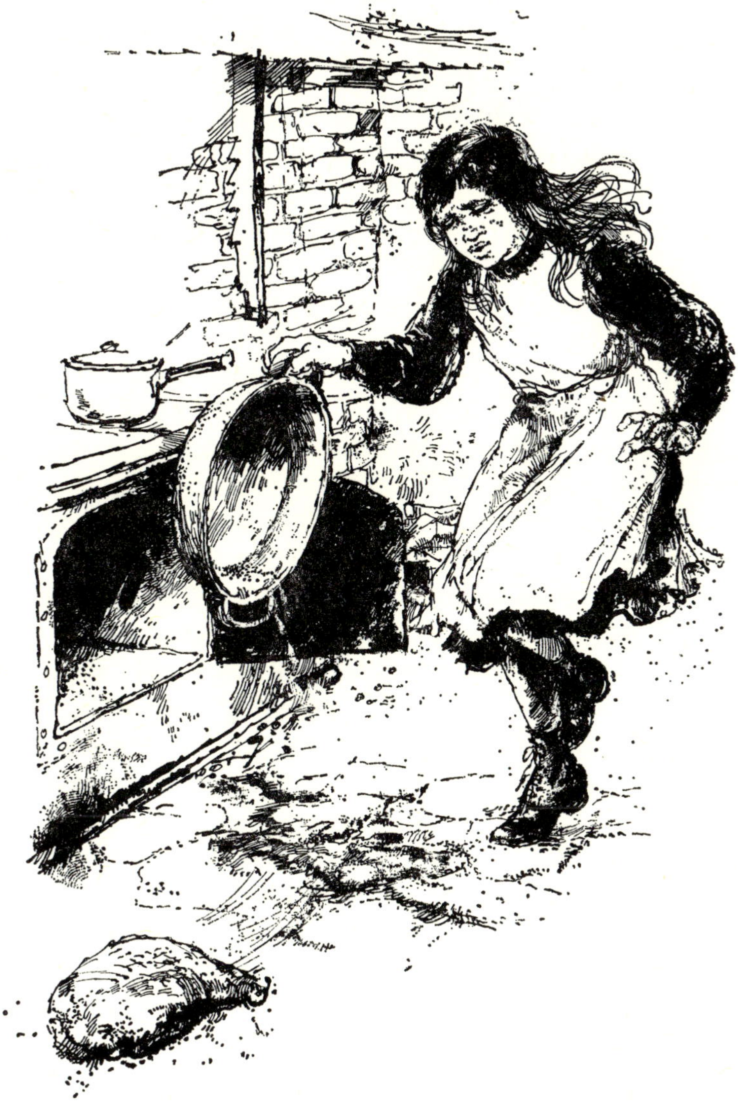

I wish to die in the pain. Then Mrs Veary give me some of the white powder, and the pain fly out the window, I seen it go, a grey thing all in rainbow round the edge. The pain go, but the room whistle round me, all jigs and jags, and all come unsteady, and in the middle of the unsteady a black bit behind my eyes and that be a sort of sleep crushing down on me. When I wake my stomach be full of curds and I drag to the garden and they pour from my mouth under the roses, and I climb back on my bed and get to sleep again.

So Saturday next I sit in the garden, and the charrybang come by with them all on, and Trombo jump down off it and come in the gate and the rest laugh at him for coming to me.

"Trombo," I said, "I never thought about nothing this whole week after I hurried this fat on my leg."

"We surmised a bit," said Trombo. "We reckon to take a fair look at old Burmouth and Sandmouth too. I be off now, Katie, or I get to walk all the way if I don't catch up the old chariot. We'll be along tonight."

So then he run along out of the garden and catch up the charrybang and climb in over the back and they drive off.

Max sent down a book to read, and it seem unkind not to scan it, but I haven't come to reading them so much, and oh dear it did look so lofty I made nothing from it. So I sit and rest, and my foot feel better and better, and by the end of the day I get in and help Mrs Veary again, though she said no need to. But well, I want to be busy out of the way of reading the book in case he ask.

My Dad come to see me during the day, passing by

with firing for home, all in leather and hot he was. He could see I moved about, so he never ask about my leg; live or dead with him is the two states, never so delicate as on the note or off like up in the church galley with the fiddle.

The charrybang was long coming. I could hardly abide the wait, but I don't want to pull it nearer, and yet I don't want to keep it off, for what is to be is just that, to be. Like Warren's two times two, have different twos and put them about, 'tis the same thing, to be, and being. So I suppose I had to know what it was to equal, and no hurry to know.

We had a lamp lit, and still no charrybang. Mrs Veary telled me it was the half of it all to come back in the dark, and maybe 'twas, but 'twas the wait of all waits, after dark.

Then it drag up, and I hear from the window, and I see the lamp on the side shake along, and come and go among the bushes, and then I see light off that lamp show the furze, and then I see it show the children on the benches, and then it come all past the garden gate and on over the heath, going down to the church gate.

I think Trombo should jump off coming back same as he did going, but none of that. Then I reckon he can't see across the dark, and then I reckon he might be sleeping in the dark, and then I think he and them all forget what they went for, only they went on a trip and might have remembered that, not about the dream.

Then I hear them across the night getting off the charrybang, and wait for someone. But no one come, nothing happen, and at last that be all for the night.

If my foot hadn't stiffed up so I might have gone across to see, but I can't hobble so far, and all I do at last is hobble to bed.

Hope deferred make the heart sick, parson say once, and true. So I never feel my leg after that, but just awaited what I awaited.

Nothing come of the morning. "I wonder how they enjoyed their day," said Mrs Veary, when she was setting off to church, for it was her Sunday for it. "You'll be sorry you didn't go, Katie Katharine."

"I be sorry not to have heard what they did," I said, and I meant more than she knew. Then off she goes, and I sit with Max for a bit, and play draughts with him, and get him books from down below, and then I come down in the kitchen again and have to look at the roast in the oven and peel up the potatoes and get greens out of the garden, until the church bell ting out twelve and then I runs down to the church, easy like on the Sunday, and pass Mrs Veary on the way home, but she walk in the lane and I went on top of the bank and I think she speak, but I don't hear.

When I got there I remembered straight off there wasn't Sunday School the day after the trip, so what a fool; but it turned out Trombo and Warren and Ruth and Susan but not Hannah was there talking under a window.

"You could have come up before," I said. "I waited the night and the morning and you never come near."

"Slept in this morning," said Trombo. "We was coming up soon."

"Not much to come up for," said Warren.

"Those two, they done nothing," said Ruth.

"They done nothing," said Susan. "But be fools in the charry."

"Out on the beach the day long," said Ruth. "We three, we went and did it all."

"Maybe," said Trombo. "It don't take all to find so little."

Those three little maids done it all, surely. They been by themselves all up and down Fore Street in Burmouth and asked in each door about Spencer.

"We thought 'twas all no, no, no," said Ruth. "Every answer wrong. We thought 'twas likely we'd be kept in after school."

"But we weren't at school," said Susan, simple maid.

"We done the whole street, and some of it was shops, and that be wrong, to ask in a shop and not buy," said Ruth.

"'Twasn't our sort of work," said Trombo that was out-and-out idle in the business.

"Then a lady come up and said she remembered the name," said Ruth. Susan said she don't understand what come next, but Ruth ask what come of Spencers, and the lady said she think they gone away after a little time, but Ruth, she don't let go so easy, and she hold on the lady and say what about the fever that year, and the lady she don't like that question.

"'Tut tut' she say," said Susan. "'Dear me, child'."

"So I say I think they be dead," said Ruth, "and the lady say not to think like that, and then she said 'twas so, they die in the fever, and then I ask her the doctor's name, and then she took us up the churchyard."

"I don't like to go in churchyards," said Susan.

" 'Tis where you are now," said Trombo.

"Well, I be going to get buried here, so," said Susan, and true it may be but no one else think so near the truth.

"They be buried there, in Burmouth," said Ruth. "There was Spencer, and just over from them was the doctor."

"Buried too," said Susan.

"Dead, maybe," said Warren, and Susan nodded.

"We can't follow them no further," said Ruth. If Susan say that then she be simpleton; if Ruth say it that be thought.

"We just ask about a girl," said Ruth. "But she hear nothing about a girl. So there be no more."

"I'll tell him," I said.

"That's his Da and his Ma," said Ruth. "You don't tell him that."

"That there be no girl I'll tell him," I said, "and then I'd to run off up to the house again for our time was over."

"He can choose now," said Trombo. "We done our part," and of course Ruth go for him then and Susan go for Warren, but I can't tidy that up. I run a bit and then I walk with my foot still sore, and come in and take Max up his dinner, and bring the tray down again. And all the time I be thinking that he can't choose that girl now, and it has to be one of us four, but likelier one of those three, and how can I bring it about and round to me?

Then I daren't come near the subject, for all I was to

tell him we cracked part of his dream and it didn't lead nowhere. I couldn't get started on it, with it all laid so close to my heart.

At the last it come easy. I'd not to start. Max begun about it round tea time. But what come out of it didn't seem good when it was begun, carried on, and finished.

"Katie," he said, "you remember my dream about the girl I want for queen."

So I begun to tell him, but his turn come first and mine never.

"You thought you had broken some of it," he said. "You knew the places in it."

"Some," I said. Then I thought that what Ruth done never got near the dream after all; that was still to come. And so.

"Katie," he said. "I want you to go down that road and to those places and break that dream for me and find her."

"Out of a dream?" I said. "Out of a dream?" And no, that couldn't be, but that be his wanting, and to be my doing.

FOUR

"Day off?" said Mrs Veary. "Why, Katie, you just took a whole week off." Maybe she give me a hard time out of not knowing what she think, and maybe she done it so it don't come too easy for me to ask time off. "And you're still hobbling about," she says.

True, that was; I should have gone lighter to the church and not fled along, for my ankle come up swelled again and the skin crack and it just bleeds.

I carry on working at her. Before I come down from Max we both think Mrs Veary isn't to hear about this dream or any further of it that we done. We'd no deceit about it, but the Troy Town game be no matter much for grown folk, and some, like the schoolmaster, don't care for it, and the parson, he reckon it might be wicked, but he have to think badly.

" 'Tis to look in the shops," I said. "Hereabouts 'tis only tinker goods and tawdry. And if I lift down on Tuesday with the carter, 'tis only half a day out of your time."

She come soft then and say that would do, and I'm glad that be cleared up, for I'm bound to go, I don't be like Trombo who complain of nothing done and go on doing it. The carter come through early on Tuesday and come back late all round about the villages.

I telled Max I'd go on Tuesday, and then he tell me the dream again. It seem about the same story, but I ask him whether he remember any more.

"It isn't remembering, Katie," he said. "It's a dream, a dream about the future. You see, I went there, and you know the way I went, so I must have walked. Walked, Katie, I walked, I shall walk if it's a true-coming dream. I could walk once, so I can again."

Well, I think, so you shall walk there if I've to carry you, but I think he might pick something ridiculous out of that and I say nothing. But at the same time I think that dream lead on to dream and his legs will never hold him, that can't be.

Tuesday I come out of bed an hour early and get the fire on and they're still asleep, and I leave all tidy and get down to the church before it ring six o'clock of a wet morning, which is what it be, and I dress myself over with a sack turned in and pixed over my head, and wait in the porch, and the rain spit down all about me, and then I hear the horse plashing on the road and go out to stop the cart.

'Twas a drear drive but dry under the tilt, and we went

roundabout, picking up goods and taking folk about, and we sit on the shelf in all the old country parcels done up rough, and, well, we get down and over the bridge, and I say to myself, here we are, when I see the painted houses, and then I get to lose track of the dream when we get in town and down towards the market square, and then I hop off and walk down a mile in the same rain to Sandmouth and the ships, where I know the dream come again.

I know it begin again here, that be all. But what way can I come up to it again ten o'clock of a wet morning and a long time since breakfast? So there I stand, looking at the water and I see nothing and 'twould be easiest walking ten miles home again and that be my resolve, only I won't do it empty. So I trail up to the marketplace and get some bread and some tea, and rest my leg up on the stall, and get cheered up, and then the sun come flop down everywhere and the rain dry, and all mist float up off the market awnings and off the cobble on the roads, and I took heart again.

It seems I love him again, but not on an empty belly, and that stay true to remember all my life. Now I've more sense, in the sunshine, and I gets on the little tram down into Sandmouth, and to the quayside again, and there was more to see.

There was the Swanston ferry coming in, black smoke and white paint and wheels like a millwheel dipping either side. I reckoned that wasn't breaking the dream, so I watch it come in and tie up and the road it made on the water smooth out and wash away and the smoke in the chimney fade away to a shimmer.

Then once more the dream break itself and no work

come to be done. A lad came by, a sailor or a fisherlad. He whistle himself along past, and then turn about.

"Ferry goes in half an hour," he said. "If that's what you're waiting for."

"To Swanston?" I said. "If that be the only place it goes, I don't want that one."

"That's the island ferry," he said. "You go about a mile that way."

Then it come to me how foolish I be, for Max said an island, but I got fixed in my mind just that the place wasn't Swanston and forgot about looking for an island.

But most dreams be folly, so breaking them has to turn that way too.

"That way," said the lad, pointing along with a nod of his head. "Is that right, the island ferry?"

"Right enough," I said, because here I be dreaming along with Max in broad daylight.

"You ring the bell," said the lad, and whistled himself off, and I could have give him a kiss.

I hanged the wet sack on a post by the sea and go on without it, looking for the island. I always think Sandmouth lie at the top of a bay and the shore run down either side, but some of that shore must be island, only I can't pick out land from land. So I trust to the island and the ferry going there, and walk along.

I come off the quay, and then past the houses, and along a road by the water. Little jetties go off into the water and the waves slop up under them and there's plenty of mud. Boats sit in the mud and there's fishermen mending nets. But I don't think I come a mile yet.

Then I think I surely have, and I don't know whether I miss the bell and should go back. But I go on and I come to a sort of gallows and there the bell do hang, and I look at it and wonder if I dare ring it. 'Twould be a prank, most times, to make it sound and run off, but my foot can't run and it think it walked far enough already.

I come up to gallows and give the rope a good twank and the bell jingle out, and I do it two more times and feel all hot with maybe doing wrong, and I stop and stand.

Then it seems not wrong but nonsense. There be a little jetty here, sure enough, but no water at it, only the same blacky yellow mud under its legs and the water a way out. So I think the sailor lad pull a joke on me, and I turn about ready to go.

Then a bell ring back at me from the other side and a man wave over there. That must be the island. He wave and shout, he shout "Wait for the tide," and I see it at once, and I know the Swanston ferry runs on the tides, early in on this one and back to Swanston and here again when the water come high, only the water don't come up here so soon, and that be what we have to wait for now.

So I wave back as if I know from always, and the man wave again, and I wait.

The water come to the end of the jetty, and then it come to the next pair of legs, and the next, half an hour creeping along, and I go out on the wood and sit at the edge until the sea touch my heels and I put my feet up again.

Then the ferry come over. It didn't get rowed, and it didn't get sailed, but had a steam chimney and came so gentle and sighing and drove up alongside and stopped. All white and red in the paint, and all golden metal shining real pretty, which is what Max said, so I be on the line of the dream still, and I wonder if I be Max dreaming it again.

A man and a woman come out of the cabin and go off ashore, and the ferryman tell me to hop on and down in the cabin, and down I go, where it be like a little house with cushions in the chairs and carpet on the floor, and I sit in a chair. The ferry huffle off backwards into the water, and then off forwards again, and I stand up, wondering what I be doing, going out off the land and beyond, the further off from England, the nearer 'tis to France.

But we end up at a jetty pretty soon, like the other, and the ferryman say this is all the way, and I get off and go up the road there past his little house. I be wondering what they talk here.

Trees growing all round me, like a forest; but one way to go, and I follow it.

Then I know the dream break. I come out in that garden he said he was in, and I know I don't dream no more myself, for I can tell I see it all real, not part of me. There's all this grass mowed off an inch high and flat, and there's trees growing up and their shadows growing along, and birds flying, and up the middle of it all there's a house, and 'tis big but tidy, old but well and all the glass bright in the sun like lit inside.

The road turn off another way and a path lead up to the house door, and I go along that, out in the sunshine. Then I think I'm not dreaming but maybe I be in the dream Max was having, for there be all this round me and me down in it, and all of it go on and on and Max dream it, and I go on and on in it, and I be me.

So I come against the house, and there be the door stood open, and I think maybe I don't show up but to me, I be not here to notice, and I go in. The hall there wink right back at me all gold and silvery and there's the fresh old chairs never used, and the fire nested up on its grate and a glass over the mantel and a hanger of ever so many candles in the roof, but not lit in the middle of the day.

I come over cold and dizzy then, and just sat on the floor by the fire a while until I get warm again, and I think I climb into my own dream a moment then for I woke, at least, if I don't sleep.

Still in the house. I standed up, and it was my foot wake me, paining me with heat of the fire so I near cry out from it. Well, that pass, and I know I be me, whatever the dream round me.

There come a noise from a doorway the other side. I think a horse stand there in its shafts, tinkling the chain in the harness like the carter's horse done all morning, but I don't know what a horse be doing in the room there, but in a dream all happens.

I hobble over, and look through the door. Now I know the dream go on, but in another day.

There they were, what Max told me. There was the young man sat down on the floor, in front of him something and it could be what I heard jangle that little bit, metals and chains. No horse in the room; there can't be with the dream breaking true like this. But up at a desk in the middle the old man with his white head of hair cutting away at somewhat with a little saw, and I stand and watch while he sets and fits pieces and then hands some down to the younger one.

Then he looks up and sees me in the doorway. I know he can't speak in the dream, but he do for all that. Or if he do then I shan't understand the talk, but I do for it be English.

"Good afternoon," he said. "Come in. What can we do for you?"

So I limp in and stand again. There be the rest of the

dream, sitting on a couch just as it was to be, the girl. She look up and see me, and pull a rug over her knees and sit, and all look at me. The girl never say a word then.

The young one on the floor climb up and stand and then pace over to me and take my elbow and put me in a chair. "Now, let's see," he said, and bobbed down on his knee and takes up my ankle. Well, I hope it can't be wrong so I say nothing, and this is no part of the dream, nothing but four folk in a room.

"Nasty little burn," he said. "You shouldn't be walking on it. But we'll give you something to ease it."

"There's no charge," said the old man. "We'd just like you to be comfortable."

So the young one go and get muslin stuff and open a jar at the back of the room and spread paste on like butter and lays it on the burn and it come comfortable and smell like the chemist.

"Is that all?" said the old one. "Is that what you came for?"

"I come about Max Spencer," I said.

The old man think a minute about that, and then he shake his head. "I don't recall the name," he said. "He isn't here now. Max Spencer? No."

I sit there a bit. I got to think how I begin to tell them how I come and what I come for. I couldn't hardly tell where to start, for it might be with the carter that morning, or it might be with Troy Town, or it might be with the dream, or with the grave up in Burmouth, and all in all it never come to me to set off about Max his own self, for here, in the middle of it all was as if he should be part of the dream breaking.

I begun somehow, but then the old one stop me. "I'd better ask the questions," he said. "First then, how did you come to hear of me?"

I tell him I don't hear so much, but Max dream him, and he shake his head at that, and I say 'tis true, and he say he believe me and my part but he don't fancy the dream end of it.

"No dream," he said. "No dream. And what's this about the carter? Now, don't hurry, just one thing at a time."

So I tell him how I come down with the carter in the rain, and got to go back at the end of the market, and where to, and he write down a few things. Then he ask about Troy Town, and write down a great deal more then, and then he say it's all by the way and might be of interest, and I tell him how Trombo come to Max and ask him to be king, but he take only little interest in that.

"And what about Max Spencer?" he said. "If he had the dream why did you come?"

"I be the serving maid for errands," I said. "And I do light the fire and keep out the donkey, and such. And I takes the little ones at Sunday School."

"But tell me about Max," he said, and I blush on that, for I can't come at a thought of Max then without it being a foolish one.

"Max be up at Mrs Veary's," I said. "We think he got no folk of his own no more."

"The grave in Burmouth," he said. "Is that it?"

So I tell him about the three girls and what they done and how Trombo done nothing, and it seem to be I shouldn't be so cross, but there, I am, poor Max all of a sudden orphan and not knowing and Trombo and Warren and David not caring when I would and I do.

"I have it all now," said the old man. "Max had the dream, and you have followed it out and found it true. Now I will tell you why it was true. First of all it is no dream. Max has been here. I do not remember him, but he must have been here. I do not know why he should remember, or dream, just now, but it seems to have something to do with Troy Town. He has sent you to follow the dream, and I think there is something you haven't told me."

"Two things," I said. For I know now I forget them when I speak.

"I know one," said the old man. "Max is paralysed."

I don't know the meaning of that, and I look at him.

"He can't move," said the old man.

"His legs," I said.

"He must come here," said the old man. "Here we can help him. These things on the bench in front of me can help him move and stand," and he lifted up the metal he had, and I see it all as black bones and leather, and I can't bear to think of them put in his legs. So I don't hear that, and I go on to tell him about the other thing.

"He dream about that girl too," I said. "How she was sat here; and 'tis she he want for queen in Troy Town time, and he say she must come up for that, for that be his choice."

"Helen," said the old man. "You would have been here. Helen of Troy: that's the link."

So then the girl speak. "He must come here," she said. "I cannot go to him," and then she look down and cry, and the young man lead me from the room and I be glad to go from the iron tongs.

FIVE

"What did you get yourself, Katie?" said Mrs Veary. I come in when she was upstairs and so I was by the fire taking a warm up when she land down.

"Nothing," I said, for that was true: I come out of that big house and down the path and over the water once more and stand under the gallows with the bell and just wonder whether I rung it or took my own dream in a blink like a fit; then I walk back into Sandmouth, pick up my sack from the post, and take the tram back up the market and wait for the carter, and that be all I done that day, to look at.

"Nothing?" said Mrs Veary. "Well, you're hard to please. I kept some tea for you," and she come to the oven where she kept something warm, she see I be holding my breath hard so I don't sob out, and I don't want her to see nothing amiss and I smile and out come breath and sob and tears and all.

I want my tea and I don't want my tea, and my head won't give over wrinkling inside and sobbing and there's my eyes running and my nose, and I take a crumb in and choke and that turn my throat twitching, but I come on through that and eat up a little, and then I be done, and nothing left of sob and tear but my throat a little oily and having to be cleared.

Mrs Veary say nothing much in all this. "Now," she said, when I had done, "tell me what's the matter, Katharine, because something is."

"There isn't nothing to tell," I said, for there wasn't nothing to tell her.

"Someone has to know," she said. "And since you came here I thought it might be me, and if it isn't then it's your mother, so out with it to me, or you'd better go home for the night with your mother."

"There be nothing to tell," I said, and just shrug up my shoulders, what the schoolmaster would call insolent.

"Never mind, Katie," she said. "I'll just walk down to your house with you, and you can come back in the morning."

I don't argue with that, for I want to be left alone, and my Mam she won't care or ask nothing.

But I forget Warren, and he be all for knowing. Then my Mam give me a whack with a wood spoon after Mrs Veary tell her some nonsense and go. My Dad rattle at the fire and say nothing.

"Looks like you be out of a place next," said my Mam.

But I don't think that; Mrs Veary and me, we get on

well. So there be only Warren, and I got nothing to say to him and no need to be kind about it, and he gets the wood fist from me and stay quiet.

Then I get to bed and sleep like all wood right through, and get out early, nothing much on my mind until I see little Hannah with the goat, and I hear the chain rattle, and I remember that same noise in the big house yesterday, and I dread me about the black bones being put in Max's legs and I go round among the furzes and won't see Hannah, but she see me and let the goat go to run after me. But I get out of speaking then.

"You foolish maid," I said, "that goat will be off on the heath all day," and I wasn't kindly to her neither, but run up to the goat and it shies off and she has to chase it and coax it, and I go to Mrs Veary's door.

I'd to wait there, however, for she hadn't come down yet. I watch little Hannah capering after the goat, and I go down and put my foot on the chain at last, and she stride off with it and won't talk, so I be through part of the day without trouble.

Mrs Veary see more than she let on about, I think. She let me in, but she forbid me to go to Max, for she say I'll upset him, and well, I be glad of that, for he'll ask about Burmouth and the dream, and I be torn of what to say. So I do my work, and every time the kettle rattle on its chain, or a knife and a fork speak together I remember the iron bones, and when I remember them I remember that proud girl too wanting him, and I can't bear either of the thoughts, and it seem that one of them get in my right hand and one in my left and I don't do nothing proper. They don't know what and where, and between them I don't neither.

My Dad come by round dinner time, but to speak to Mrs Veary, which they do for a moment at the gate, but nothing for me, and she say nothing too, so I don't ask. Maybe I am to lose my place here, and that be the third twist in the braid.

Then I be in the garden later, shifting weeds out of the soft soil after the rain, when Trombo come along.

"Warren got a bruise on him," he said.

"You too," I said, and I wave the hoe at him, so he stop out in the road and talk over the hedge.

"What did you find down to Burmouth?" he said.

The solving come to me without thinking, and I hadn't to get off the truth. "Best find another king," I said. "That'll clear that."

"We don't like to do that," said Trombo, but I can tell he mean it be the best thing after all, and I think that be settled, and so it would be if David and Warren didn't come up after him then.

"She find something out yesterday," said Warren, and the hoe isn't long enough to hit him over the hedge.

"We can get another king," said Trombo.

"She ain't like a wild heath cat for nothing," said Warren. "She found out only she won't say."

I don't know what Warren might be out with next. But 'twas David with the question.

"What did he say?" he asked, and he mean Max, nodding his head up to the windows the wrong side of the house.

He haven't said nothing, Max haven't, for I never see him, so there be nothing to say. So I weed on a bit and they look over the hedge. Then in a bit they come round to the gate and through, and start to pick out weeds with their fingers, and before long there's Ruth, and Susan who pull off the tops and leave the roots, and then Hannah, and together we weeds ten time as fast as I do alone and the job be done.

Then I think, 'tis the foolish one Susan pulls out the tops and leaves the root, and me, I be another foolish one, pulling off the tops of my thoughts and leaving the weeds, and with all of us together 'twas like at school when I was there.

"I hope not to tell it twice," I said. "We'll go on in and tell it to Max," and we do that, only Mrs Veary put us all at the kitchen sink to water away the garden dirt from our hands. Then she takes us up, and announce another deputation.

This time Max be well. No troubles or pain on him today. We stood about him, and 'twas a roomful of folk and he make them all sit on the floor and I take my chair.

"There wasn't any flowers," said Susan. "I looked but 'twas all thistles," and that account for the way she weed a garden, picking flowers she was.

"I've been waiting for you, Katie," said Max. "Why didn't you come?"

"I broke the dream," I said. "And I can't bear to say how 'twas, I can't bear to think for you how it might be, Max."

"I sent you, so you must tell," said Max.

"Yes," I said.

"There was a bell to ring for the ferry," he said. "It came to me later."

" 'Twas no dream," I said. "I walked on along the shore and rung that bell, and a boat come across for me and I come to the island."

"Trees," said Max. "All trees."

"Then the garden," I said. " 'Twas still a dream then."

"Talk about real," said Hannah. "I don't like a living dream."

" 'Tis real," I said. "I went in the house but 'twas like a dream then, and I never knock or ring a bell, and then I find the hall with the gold and silver and the fire, and then I go through a door and there be the young man."

"There should be two young men," said Max.

" 'Twas only one," I said. " 'Twas no dream, 'tis how it was yesterday."

"He should be playing a game," said Max. "But he can't alone."

"He had 'somewhat' in his hands," I said. "And there was the old man up in the middle of the room."

"That's right," said Max.

Then Hannah gets up and runs from the room and clatter down the stairs, and we wait a minute, for Mrs Veary come up in her place.

"What's going on?" she asked. "What's the matter with Hannah, running off like that?"

" 'Tis a fancy she've took, "said Trombo. "Terrible fanciful, is Hannah."

"You're sure you're not all being fanciful?" said Mrs Veary, and she looks at Max, but nothing wrong with him. And she look at me, but nothing wrong with me neither.

"I wish them to stay, thank you Mrs Veary," said Max, and I can't speak to her like that or I'd get boxed, but it come natural to Max. Then he look at her until she go, and she go.

"The old man," said Max.

"Making things, like you said," I said, and don't want to say no more. I remember it was bad.

Max remember the same. "I didn't like it," he said.

"No more did I," I said, and we leave that there in silence a bit, and go on to the next.

"And the girl?" said Max.

Then we both speak together, and say "Helen", and

Ruth don't like that, for hope's gone, and I don't, but me and Ruth be together in this, not on other sides like we were, so we look at each other and don't move nor think. We all lost then, and no more to be said, except what the girl say when I leave yesterday, and that can't be.

"Helen," said Max again. "I knew it could break." And then we drop off her a bit and get back to the old man and what he was doing.

"There's the bit I don't like," said Max. "What is it; what was he doing?"

I hold on a bit and then I come out with it. "Making terrible black iron bones to put in your legs and make you walk," I said.

"I can't walk," said Max. "Nobody ever says it, but I know."

"We know," said Trombo.

"But I could once," said Max, and he pulls back his cover and there's his legs lying down in the bed, and I get up and pull the cover on again, and there's tears down my face but I don't sob, just run over with them and sniff. One eye is for loving Max, and the other for the terror of the iron bones, and never a thought about being queen to him, for I see that this Helen won't come to him, and he can't never in the world get down there, and isn't to think of it.

So I be easy when he ask about the girl again, but before that 'tis the bones once more.

"I don't think they would be any good, Katie," he said. "And I don't like them any better than you do."

Then I tell him I ask the girl whether she will come up and be queen, and Ruth's eyes waken, for she would be glad for the girl to come, out of romance, or for her not to and get another chance herself.

"Will she?" said Max. "I expect not, or you would have come before and told me."

"You must go to her," I said. "That's what she tell me."

"Well then," said Max, "I'll have to go."

I thought to let that tumble about in his mind a bit until he see it can't be. We'd have to come at it again and get it blunted off a bit before he would give it up. So I was going to talk of the painted ferry boat, but Ruth said, "That's more than we found out from the lady in Fore Street."

"She just took us to your Da and Ma's grave," said Susan, the great clumsy-speaking thing she is.

"I want to see that too," said Max, and then I knew

with the two things together he was bound to be off. So Max tell us to fit the journey up for him, and we all go out from the room and come down stairs.

"In my own house," said Mrs Veary, "I don't know what's going on. What is it, Katharine?"

"I'll just go down to my Mam's," I said, and so I did but the long way about, for I don't want my Mam of course, but my Dad, for he'll do what I do say. And lose my place or not, I be bound to do what Max say, not what Mrs Veary say, though I don't wish to vex her.

Not the next day, but the next day after the school bell rung extra long, for the top pupils never come in school at all that day, Trombo and David and Warren and the three girls. They come up Mrs Veary's instead, and my Dad come too, and they wheel the donkey cart on but no donkey.

"Just a little ride for the boy," say my Dad, for that be what he think, just to Troy Town and back, and that be how we begin, Troy Town being along our way.

Max get settled comfortable as he can, which it be not always easy to find. I take on the bottle of white powder and a pitcher of water and the cup and the spoon.

"Well, I hope 'tis all right," said Mrs Veary, and she stay back to turn out the room and air the mattress, and we all set off. My Dad don't know, only us and Max, we know.

So we come on to Troy Town and look at that, and my Dad done most of the pulling along. And then we had him pulling again, but we never went back home, we went on over the heath and my Dad get told as he goes what we be about, and he say he be the biggest donkey ever in those shafts.

We cross the heath, and Max is happy still. "I am managing very well," he said, but I think he might be pale, but then he stay in his room all day and that make him waxy to start.

We get on the good road at the end of the heath, and down along that way, dropping down the hill.

"This is the road in the dream," said Max, and Hannah think she might go home then, not liking the mixture, but Max take her up in the cart a bit and tell her 'twas only remembered like a dream, and she settle a bit.

Up and down hill we went, and each was bad, push up the hill and hold back down, 'twas all work, and we can't stop or we never start again.

Max in a bit, but we'd come better than half way, close his eyes and get a bit of a headache, but he might have that any day. Then he get a pain down his back, but by then we see the bridge ahead, and when we get near to it I get up in the cart and mix him up some powder and he take that, but it do nothing for him.

When we come to the bridge he said, "I think I'll die," and I say we'll stop, but he won't hear that and tell us to go on and take him down dead if we must.

So we go on, and 'tis worse and worse for him and he can't sleep but he get sick, and my Dad say, "Oh God, we kill him we come to be blamed," and Max said "No, no, go on, go on," so we go on down Burmouth, and Max say, not to stop but go slow by the church, and Ruth run up in the churchyard and stand by that grave, and I wipe his mouth and let him look, and we go on, and when he speak again he say to bury him there too.

My Dad pull on, enough breath left in him to say all the time he be a murderer, and we pull down to Sandmouth and along the shore and 'tis a bad road and I can't tell, I think Max die then, his breathing stop, and we come to the ferry and ring the bell, and Max stir, and I think that be the last time I'll see him move.

The ferry come, and we lift him down in the cabin, and the ferryman don't fuss, he just say we come too late, and we all think that too, but he give us a bear to bear him along at the other side and we come in the house and to that room and my Dad all a pother about walking in, and we put Max on the floor and the old man start up, and the young one and the girl there all eating their dinners and the knives jangle like iron bones.

And Max open his eyes and look about and say "Helen," and she don't move, and Max reach up and take my hand but he can't speak and he drop it again and can't speak, and close his eyes.

SIX

Max die so many times, I see him go that much, I know he must have gone this time for sure, and so do the old man and the young one.

"Best go and wait out in the hall," said the young one, and we come out one way and they go out another bearing Max on the bear, and the girl sitting there saying no more, I would have jumped up and done somewhat, but I don't, I come out with the rest and sit on a chair built to look at. I don't do nothing.

Trombo sit by the fire and take off his boots and dry the sweat out of his feet. My Dad stand by the window and the floor be so shiny he stand the other way up in that too, and nobody say nothing about anything.

A long time go by, best part of an hour, but I don't see the clock standing there, like my Dad the other way up in that bright floor, until it ding out three o'clock, and then after that it pick pick pick all the time so I wonder why I ever think it quiet in there.

Then the younger man come in. "Are you the father?" he said to my Dad.

"Just of two of them," said my Dad.

"Not of the boy you brought?" said the man.

"Is he dead?" I said, and Ruth said "He's dead," together.

"One at a time," said the man. "The boy is well and asleep; don't worry about him. But we want to know who he is."

Who he be don't matter to me, but alive and well mean a lot, and I get out from the chair and into the garden and walk about on that clipped grass and tears run down inside my nose but not out of my eyes, and I'll be glad always of that moment, for I see myself at the end of foolish fancy but love him just as much and maybe better, and I love his queen too and hope all I can for them both. I come out of my passion for him, and 'twasn't love before, 'twas foolishness like Mrs Veary said, and like I say to myself, but better to be foolish first and wise after than another way about.

Hannah come out for me in a bit, and we went through the house to the back in the kitchen and they give us some tea, the cook there, and my Dad laugh with the cook and say he'll stop down here and daren't go back on the heath after what we done, and then in a little after that the cook brisk us all out the door and we come round the road and down to the ferry again, and there be our donkey cart tipped up the far side of the water, and the ferryman brisk us on the ferry off the end of the jetty and put us on the end the far side for the water be low.

We run the cart off the road on the grass and walk on to Sandmouth and take the tram up the town and then we've to walk back home.

That was a long drudge, and dusk when we got up on the heath, and dark when we came in among the houses and Ruth sleep on my Dad's back and stopping asleep when her Mam lift her down at the door.

"I won't say nothing," she said. "But there be something I have to hear, and you best go up and see Mrs Veary."

"You young 'uns go home," said my Dad. "Katie and I has to face the music to Mrs Veary's."

There was some music that night. Mrs Veary play the whole band at us, and my Dad biding quiet like he do, and me thinking of that empty room above. She want to know all, how, why, where, when, who and which and whatever and all the whither and whence and she don't stop to hear none of it but go on about Max and no one cared but she herself and about getting the constable in the morning, and she never want to see neither of us again, and then she send me off to my bed and call my Dad a great fool and talk on some more. Then he go, and she bring me a candle and a cup of tea and hold my hand and cry and cry but I be beyond crying, and I hold her tight like she was Max herself and the tea grow cold and I come out of bed and we make more tea and build up the fire and sit there like it was winter drinking it.

In the morning she take off for Burmouth. She be bound to go, she say, and I say she might have come yesterday, and she say she might have but she wouldn't have let us go. So I get the house to myself, and it never was empty before with no Max in it, and every time I think of him I think I give him my thought, not like it was before when I pull from him every time I think of him.

Warren come up in the afternoon. The schoolmaster took and beat them all, so he can't stand for blisters on his feet, and he can't sit neither. The schoolmaster think to stop the Troy Town lark, he say, but it be out of school time and he can't. Our Dad took a bit from our Mam too, out of talking to Mrs Veary all night. I be the one with no hurt, I be the one that come out more comforted, but for my ankle swelling out again a little. And I hope Max rise up better too.

Mrs Veary come in late herself, all her petticoat dragging in mud from getting out of the ferry.

"I've been there, where Max is," she said. "How you came to the place I don't know. I never heard of it before. Do you know what they do there?"

"Put black bones in Max's legs," I said, but it come to me then that Max has to care about that, not me, and if he come with a black iron head on him I still got him safe and I still love him but it don't hurt me no more.

"I saw him," said Mrs Veary. "They have a little infirmary there, and there he was laid. But we'll have our tea now."

Mrs Veary and I we don't get much work to do now there be no Max to look after. She think I might have to

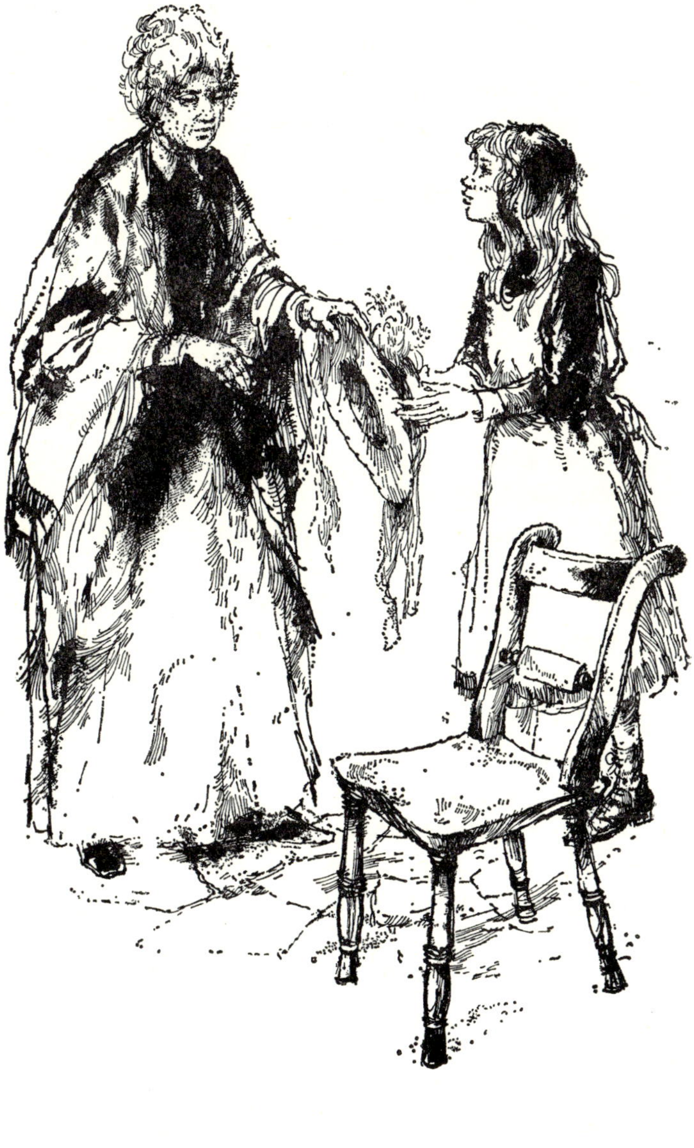

lose my place, if she were sensible, but I don't want to go, and she don't want to be all alone, so I stay a bit and stay a bit, and time go by.

Trombo and the others, they wonder too about the time going by. Trombo come up one day and he don't like to get off the path, for we've worked the garden so hard 'tis like a carpet, so neat. Trombo he come about the Troy Town.

"We haven't got no king, it seem," he said. "We had him, and we see the queen, and nothing heard any more. He didn't die, or like that, did he?"

"Mrs Veary seen him," I said, for she'd seen him that once and then another time when she go down with the carter. "Still abed, he is."

"I walked down far enough last time," said Trombo. "I could send one of they little maids, maybe."

"I never hear so idle," I said.

"You ha'n't been down neither," said Trombo, and I hadn't, true. However, Trombo think he might write a letter, and Mrs Veary give us the address. A day go by, and a day, and Trombo write nothing, and I tell him again how idle, and another day and another, and at last more idle, for 'tis little Hannah come up with a letter one day that she'd wrote and wanted the address, for Trombo lose that. I think Trombo want some ordering up one of these days. So, well, we send the letter off, and there come a reply all the way to Hannah, and I'd be wild one time at that, but now 'twas right, she wrote the letter.

The letter say that king and queen be going on well and would be up at midsummer to Troy Town. 'Twas a strange letter, like from really royal, but Mrs Veary she laugh and say that Max be joking at us and it show his good health.

Trombo think to write back then, but Warren bring me the letter, and it only said "If you come," and then a blot, and that be all of Trombo in writing and ink. So I get a letter written to Max and tell him his room be all ready and the garden fine and we got a cat now in case he don't come again, and I tell him all Trombo's little message. I get a reply back out of Max, saying he's going on well and not to worry about the black bones, it isn't what I think, and I haven't to visit him, though I never know I can, because I wouldn't like it, but he don't say why, and he add a little bit for Trombo which say And if I come, and a bit for me which is he will come at midsummer.

Mrs Veary get down to the place again in the beginning of June. She come back glad and sad, for, she say, if she knew before how he could have come on she would have had him down there, but the way he was was only crippled and not ill, and never had a doctor near that might have told her.

Then come midsummer. For all he say he won't the schoolmaster let the school off the day, and there was a holiday for all, and we went to Troy Town and mended up the banks and cleaned up in the ditches, and the donkey come along with the cart, now it come up from the shore, and there was straw in the cart and 'twas spread about for folk to sit or lie on in the dances. Then there was firings for a beacon got ready, and the schoolchildren had races in the road and charrybangs come from other villages, and a trap or two from curious folk belonging away and the pie stall man out of Burmouth market come along and the photographist from Sandmouth, and the innkeeper brought a barrel early in the day and covered it in a wet sack to keep the cider cool.

"No sign of the king and queen yet," said Trombo. "We'll have to pick. It might be you yet, Katie."

"You been at the cider, young Trombo," I said; but I got no bother with the thought of being queen or not, 'tis all even with me now it be fixed up, and besides I don't feel so personal with Max, but I think that be after the number of times he died and it don't kill me each time.

But whatever my heart say, my knees get all quivery as time go by and I await and await and no one come up from Burmouth but the pie man and the photographist and so on. And now the place be so milled with children out of all the villages I can't tell who be who, and our lot so brushed up and tidy I don't know Warren when he knock into me and miss a chance of hitting him thinking he be a stranger until he get out of reach.

Well, I wouldn't hit, but I be so stretched inside I can't stand still, for I want to know how Max come on down there, and how he'll be, and still no sight of him.

Teatime come first, and we all sit down on the straw but me, and I sits on some furze that Trombo put under me, but I can't do with chasing him about like children, I be older than that. Mrs Veary come over the straw and sits by me, and we eat a little, for the fire-side supper come at dark, and that be a good while off yet.

A wagon come up from the road, but only more children from the far side, no king or queen.

"They'll be here about seven," said Mrs Veary. Well,

I don't know seven from twelve out on the heath here, so I get no help from that. Farmer Cantle, Ruth's grandpa, have the watch and keep order of time for this and I don't speak to him in his funeral hat.

Mrs Veary says I got time to trip back home with the

basket now and save carrying it later, so I take it back, and all the houses be empty, and ours emptiest still, the village be haunted with nobodies, and I run back in case they come out and see me, and in case I miss out on the king and queen, Max and the girl.

Now there come games for the children, and I sit and watch this year.

"Go and join in," said Mrs Veary. "You're still a child." But I say no, for I been in love and they only think they have and that make me different.

But I watch the games and enjoy that, and I could just see myself at some times being one of them. In the middle of it all Farmer Cantle look in his watch and the innkeeper drive in the spigot in the barrel and lift the spile in the bung and draws cider for the men, but Trombo don't get any, little devil.

The games run out, and the children begin to get gathered up in parties and little flocks, and go off into the furze and get their costume on. Just on a sudden I wonder what Max and his queen wear, but Mrs Veary say the man in Sandmouth know it all and I don't have to fret. Then there's skirmishings and shoutings when the boys slide over to watch the girls, and then all's ready but the time, and it isn't time yet. I see Farmer Cantle shake his head when he look in his watch. Then Susan come clump over a thick straw and roll over in the ditch of Troy Town and show her drawers and the boys cheer and Susan cry and pout.

Then a sprung wagon come up the road, and there be no sprung wagon in our villages on the heath. On it sit the old man and the young one, and in the back a nurse, and down, lying small, Max, and beside him another head, and my heart go bang but not like it go bang in the old days, for, well, I share him now, and 'tis bang to see him, not bang to jealous him.

The wagon come right up on the straw, and folk clear from the way and stand forward and get sent back and the horses sniff the straw and won't touch it. The side of the wagon come down, and the young man lift Max off it, and he look round I hope to see me, and whatever sense come to me leave me then and I go to him and folk get out of the way and pat me on the back but why I don't know, I be no queen, and Max say "Hello Katie" and I look at him and I be pleased with how they keep him down there and he take my hand again but this time he go on living, carried off by the man, Farmer Cantle leading the way, and they step over and step over to the middle of Troy Town, Farmer and the two men and king and queen, and set them in the place, and Max, he sit up without a cushion at his back, which he never done before.

The wagon be got out of the way by then, and the dance start, with my Dad leading on the fiddle for the music, and they rant on down along the maze, in and out, some of them up and some of them down, and at the last Trombo does it nice for all he's a fool, and him and Ruth end up alongside king and queen and set the crown on their heads, and that be the first dance.

The second dance come a tumble part way through, but I never knew it didn't, and they get a clap from us all and start again and get it right all the way, and get a bigger clap and I know how they feel.

Then they refresh and the beacon get lighted. Mrs Veary and I we wonder how Max get to sit up so long when he never done it at all before, and we think how we done wrong all this time and not made him. But I found out how soon, for before the music start for the last dance the young man go out to Max and the girl to see how they fare, and they fare well, we see them smile.

"It'll be the white powder for him tonight," said Mrs Veary. "I wonder he smiles now."

Then the young man come over to me. "He wants you to go out there with him for the last one," he said.

"He got a queen," I say, but I don't hold back, and go across.

"I'll stand for this dance, Katie," he said. "We both

will. But we can't quite do it alone yet, so be between us."

"I'll stand just behind," I said.

"Lift me," he said, and I lift him, and he was never so heavy, and I found what held him; I found the iron bones.

"They put them outside, Katie," he said. "I take them off, and I can stand."

The girl come up easier, she hold her crown on while I grab her up, and all three of us stand and the music begin, and they lean on me, and the two of them hold hands.

"Hold hands too, Katie," said Max, and there we be, all three clung together and the last rant came all about us and the smoke off the beacon, and now I think they both be mine.

Max come up better and better after that, and the girl Helen too. I went in their service later and we live in London, where they need a strong girl, for they never come apart until Max die the last time a grown man, a Member of Parliament, and she go too not long after, and I come back on the heath and find Trombo still idle and take him in hand, and I seen him go by too, I be bound to see them go by living into my nineties. I don't walk myself no more, but there'll come a day when I gets lifted up and stands again, so I be content.